Anna Matlack Richards

Dramatic Sonnets

Anna Matlack Richards

Dramatic Sonnets

ISBN/EAN: 9783337334321

Printed in Europe, USA, Canada, Australia, Japan

Cover: Foto ©Andreas Hilbeck / pixelio.de

More available books at **www.hansebooks.com**

DRAMATIC SONNETS

A.M.R.

In truth the prison unto which we doom
Ourselves, no prison is: and hence to me
In sundry moods, 'twas pastime to be bound
Within the sonnet's scanty plot of ground
Pleased if some souls, (for such there needs must
Who have felt the weight of too much liberty [be)
Should find brief solace there as I have found.

WORDSWORTH

PREFACE.

FOR the sake of thoughtful readers to whom the name "Dramatic Sonnets" may not explain the contradictory nature of the various forms of opinion to be found in them, it is well to say; that these verses are part of an unfinished design to give expression to every possible form of conflicting thought and feeling.

Only occasionally, is there any meaning observed in the order of sequence.

A.M.R.

1

LET not Theology, nor Sentiment—
That half interpreter of truths, be bold
To speak of things that Faith alone can hold
Of right divine, and yet be ill content
That Art should dare invade her element:
Art the grave master with clear vision cold.
And heart of warmest love for the manifold
Converging forces that in truth are blent.
Religion hath no science and no form
But in the silent world of Faith; and we
Who would create her image, must employ
The unsparing hand of Art; all night and storm
And fear that shape her outlines, we must see
No less than her indwelling light and joy.

EARTH'S highest gift, be others what they may
Is leisure—measured duty, needful care,
But time for thought. Alas, not everywhere,
Have duty's keenest followers won the day;
For the unresisted impulse to obey
The prompting of a thoughtless conscience, bare
To every sting, must the firm will impair,
And waste our strength in labyrinths far away
From simple action. Master of his soul
Is he whom careful Nature hath endowed
With power to stay, and let the world go by,
The worlds conflicting duties past him roll,
Till he discern, from all the tumult loud
The single voice with warrant from on high,

Recluse by nature, or from circumstance
Or wise resolve,—we, who long solitude
Have chosen, where the world may not intrude;
Let us from strength to higher strength advance
Nor be content with peace that any chance
Of man's regard, that needless gratitude
For recognitition menace, still renewed
Through new rebellion. Their serene expanse
Of birthright freedom, they alone, indeed
Inherit, who to the sovereignty are born
Of mortal envy; who from life recede
Not out of ignorant hate, nor thoughtless scorn,
But from allegiance to a higher creed
That social laws and duties have forsworn.

No peace that grants a haven of repose
From Earth's incessant vanity and care
But must be dearly purchased. All men share
The struggle for existence, and even those
Who tired of life's conventions, empty shows
And heartless triumphs, in themselves will dare
Resolve to live above them, must prepare
For other conflicts, though with other foes.
The world will rally to avenge the cause
Of her elect, and in what fortress rare
Of self-possession we may scorn to fear
The onset, she will claim for broken laws
Indemnity in secret, hard to bear
 As the exactions of her vexed career.

LORD, I believe; help thou mine unbelief,
Or teac' ·· that it weighs not in thy scale
A grain of dust. Although my vision fail,
Although this world stand in so bold relief
Against thy far pale heaven, though ages, brief
Yet self-sustaining in their tenure frail
Make life eternal but an idle tale,
Lord, I believe; help thou mine unbelief.
Assure me of the truth I only feel,
That doubt is but an ailment of the mind
That life may heal; a burden of the soul
That patience lightens, though until the seal
Of Death is raised, my conscience waits to find
That faith whereof no dogma hath control.

DENY thy heart the false humility
That claims the merciful justice God and man
Accord to ignorance, thou, in Nature's plan
The first and last, to whom the truth is free
As air and light. The freedom that must be
To acknowledge heights and depths we cannot span,
And limitations that with thought began,
Confound not with the slothful liberty
Of uncontrolled conscience, that may choose
Its own false limit, intercepting light
To boast of doubt and darkness that refuse,
That fear,decision, while to left and right
The radiance of thy nature's inward sun
Shines on thy vineyard's work, unloved, undone.

I, TURNING from my faith to Knowledge, saw
All forms of life go down to endless death,
Nor was there power in man's diviner breath
To stay the arm of universal law.
And when I said that man must surely die,
Behold my living soul was dead within;
He crucified afresh who for my sin,
Did once draw near the mercy seat on high.
Ah! Lord my soul is dead, my heart is cold,
That did aspire to serve thee night and day,
Ah! cruel hands have taken my Lord away
That I nor love nor fear Him as of old.
And to these prayers that fill the vacant skies
No Voice in all the universe replies.

So dear is life, and the beloved dust
That answers to our love no more, so dear,
That the unconscious argument, sincere,
Of strong desire may build the innate trust
In life immortal. Even the hosts august,
Martyr and saint and ministering angel, clear
To wistful faith, fade from his atmosphere
Who finds eternal Nature wisely just
In death as life, who loves the truth so well,
That life is not so dear. Although the law
Of visible Nature may not mark the tide
And limit of the will of God, nor tell
The tale of being, with no lessen'd awe
He bows, who dares to otherwise decide.

From that calm height where Law can never yield
His place to Mercy, comes to mortal ears
The cry, Renounce! that every one who hears
Must, as he will, interpret. On some field
Of that self-warfare they are called to wield
A sword of fire, whose names are written clear
Whether in heaven or earth; and in the sphere
Of every life, however man may shield
His slothful will, the unexplained command
Haunts the convictions of his troubled mind
With dreams of rest. It may be that we live
Upon the borders of a promised Land,
Where the obedience of the Law would find
A recompense that Mercy cannot give.

OF all the spoils of victory Life recounts
Is it then true that nothing is her own.
And that by restoration she alone
To the fulfilment of possession mounts?
Is then that voice of martyr deeds, Renounce!
The only key to victory they have known
Who have the stronghold of the will o'erthrown
And drink of power from superhuman founts?
Ah, even such victory may be dearly bought.
And such possession, loss! O, life, no more,
Even for those glimmering principalities,
Give up the birth-right of thy freeborn thought;
Nor vex the sunshine of thy native shore
With dreams that rove the dark surrounding seas.

HERE, where not always we behold the race
Unto the swift, we, who by random gift
Of careless Nature, are among the swift
And strong ennumbered, must assert our place
Of strongest, often, by the patient grace
That bears with failure. There is power to lift
The soul of man from those dark tides that drift
Despair and death to meet him, in the face
Of his own mercy. Ah, the task is light
To grow impatient with ourselves, to scorn
Our poor absolving,—hard indeed to fight
The self-condemning from self-knowedge born,
But he is strongest who can most forgive
To that lost youth he never can relive.

I, WHO am young, let me not crave too much
The burden of content, not too much strain
The shining mirage of Desire to touch:
Fruition's rest is full of nameless pain.
And yet, O End! O Rest! if there be such
In all the world, come in the mighty reign
Of autumn on this silent inland plain,
Unto a spirit toiling over much.
I, who am old, let not my heart annul
By futile hope the gain of suffering years,
Nor make the fine gold of their wisdom dull
With youth's sweet passion of unfruitful tears.
And yet, in this fair Spring, with Nature's tongue,
I cry aloud, would God, I too were young.

WHEN they who sleep the sleep of youth awake,
And first discern how grievous was their fault
To dream that passion might their lives exalt
Above the never-changing laws that make
Eternal change prevail, they cannot break
The chain of hope. Although their courage halt,
They ever more must arm to the assault
Of some fierce stronghold, none may ever take.
Hope ! thou who dost our morning prayer uplift.
And at the eventide forsakest thy trust,
Ah, take the treacherous anchor from their souls !
Better with winds and currents of nature drift,
Better in deep sea calms of knowledge to rust,
Than to be moored in tidal depths and shoals.

THOUGH thou hast learned the lesson of the years.
And mastery over ignorance, that brings
The deep relations of discordant things
To make the harmony of the living spheres ;
Though from out earth and heaven unto thine ears
Unfold their magic awful, viewless kings
That reign in mountain summits and the rings
Of the vast seas ; yea, though thy spirit hears
Nature herself, the voice of God, the word
Which is the Life, if love for thine own kind—
So easily lost, so hard to keep or find—
Abide not with thee, all that thou hast heard,
All thou hast seen cannot redeem thy soul;
Thou art no part of life's immortal whole.

THOU who dost sit among us at the hearth ,
Thou also wast with Him of Galilee,
The virgin-born ;— thy speech betrayeth thee :
And fearing the encounter of their mirth ,
I , who above all the dearest things of earth
Have held Him dear, made answer sorrowfully :
I know Him not ; nothing is He to me—
Nothing the world-tradition of His birth.
Then to the Christ within my soul I said:
(Hoping that Simon's grace might still be mine)
Dear Lord, to men like these can I lay bare
The mystic union that with thine has wed
My secret life? The Spirit made no sign;
Christ heard me not, He was no longer there.

New teachers of the world, whose liberal thought
Would mould the weak and timid of our race
In new heroic forms of inborn grace,
And buy for them the truth that is not bought,—
Have ye not learned what miracle were wrought.
If, with their swift temptations face to face,
The expedient lie could lightly yield its place,
Or inward honor were by teaching taught?
The minds that can of everything discern
The intrinsic worth, that feel the subtle line
Dividing truth from falsehood, have no need
Of human words, but who the truth must learn
Would counterfeit her likeness with desire
To steal the birthright of a nobler breed.

CEASE brave Philosophy,— and even thou
Religion, with what heavenly warrant pure,—
Who waste our strength in warfare to secure
Impossible peace . Stoic, or saint ! avow
That ye, whom definite griefs at last endow
With calm of resignation, have no cure
For those who must a life suspense endure,
Where Hope's uncertain tides no pause allow
For that despair named patience. Let us find
A peace that need not on our hopes depend,
Days with absorbing thought and action filled,
In which the invincible sorrows of the mind
No more with that perpetual present blend
That man above his past may ever build.

So long as in the starry fastness cold,
Where force and matter join in swerveless law,
A power unknown is throned, so long as awe
Must grow with growing knowledge, and untold
The mighty secret of their life enfold
The living, so long will the star they saw
That led them to the young child Jesus, draw
The wise men toward him, and no man withhold
A Savior human and divine. Fear not,
O small Evangelist, truths like these have been
In peril of loss. That God came down from heaven,
Will be a legend ever unforgot
Through the remotest ages, while men sin
Against themselves the seventy times of seven.

WE have not lived in vain who see at last
The all loving God has known us, year by year,
That he rejoiced with us in that dear past
Wherein we did not dream that he was near;
Nor did refuse our hopeless call to hear.
When, high enthroned in starry spaces vast,
He seemed so far from the remorse and fear
Of mortals from their paradise outcast.
He sent His ministering angels, patient Time,
And Wisdom, that compel us to outlive
The death of youth. O Father ! since that prime
Of grief is past, let thy strong angels give,—
Not the forgetfulness of loss alone,
But of the joy whose loss we have outgrown.

THE sun has risen above the wide, grey beach,
The day is fair,— the morning brings a thrill
Of hope and courage, and more resolute will
The narrow way of higher life to reach.
Shall not some newborn power of thought or speech
This day the earnest dreams of faith fulfil,—
Transcend our thoughts of relative good and ill
By some eternal truth, defining each
With clearness no expedients that assail
Weak wills can darken? Oh, to be only sure
Of absolute right, and never more to quail
Before a tutored conscience, nor to endure
The weight that other men's convictions give
Our fears, life would be easier far to live.

GOD speaketh and saith; "I do remember thee
When thou wentest after me in the wilderness:
No desert could withhold thee, no distress
Of drought or fire, no perils of land or sea
Could come between thy burning love and me;—
Where art thou now?" Ah, Lord, the world did press
With love more dear than thine to save and bless,
With life more near than thy eternity,
With promise more than all the world could fill;
O, that I might return to thee, before
The latest days, before my heart is cold!
"Return,—I will have mercy on thee still
With everlasting kindness; but no more
Canst thou draw near with that same love of old."

"COME now and let us reason," saith the Lord:
Nor more transcendent reason can we know,
Than that our scarlet sins shall be as snow;
That justice yields no ground, when her accord
With perfect mercy, stays the righteous sword
That spares our guilty souls. The heavens glow
With one consuming fire of love; and though
Inflexible memory never hath restored
A stainless past, and though experience, wise
With lessons of our folly, may refuse
A stainless future, to the spirit within,
Where God's eternal boundless present lies,
Is neither past nor future : Life may choose
Each moment new existence to begin.

24

WE must be born again. What they may mean,
Who spake of blood and water, and the swift
Fire of the spirit, though we may not lift
Our faithless eyes to see, we cannot screen
The indwelling sin; nor mists of pride, between
Our thought, and knowledge of the truth can drift,
That we, unless we may accept some gift
Of infinite repentance, are unclean
For evermore. No purgatorial fire,
No graded progress through celestial spheres
Hath logic to persuade the world, that sin
Hath not immortal guilt, nor that desire
Can take away that life's remaining years
From some regeneration might begin.

25

Know, thou who seest the havoc life has made
In some false soul, that once was true and fair,
Not more to thee is all the ruin laid bare,
Than to itself, not less of thine afraid,
Than its own condemning. Ah, betrayed
Of creeping habit,—Nature's cunning snare
For hearts that trust her,—who can tell what pray-
Has cried to Nature's God too late to aid!   [er,
"My yoke is easy, and my burden light:"
But one who his own burden long hath borne,
Who has the yoke of this world too long worn,
Loves not the freedom of the inward might:
Youth, with its ardent fire of self-control,
Alone hath will, hath power to exalt the soul.

26

Is it thou who knowest no faith, who hast no dread
Of the Nemesis of life? Thou fool, before
Thine eyes she stands, the threshold of thy door
She enters even now with noiseless tread;
And ever when thou layest down thy head,
She is it, whom thou dost in vain implore
To call the illusions of the past once more,
And for these stones give back their living bread.
Thou knowest her not,—thee she has always known,
Ever pursuing, neither in sorrow nor wrath,
Thy footsteps, nor in kindness, but alone,
In silence, where thou hast ordained her path:
Mercy has no such power in the boundless heaven
As thou thyself to Nemesis hast given.

27

STERN, narrow soul, lost in the vague domain
Of mystic faith; strong will by accident
Of birth, that urged by heavenly discontent
The impossible heights of perfect peace to gain
Didst not prevail beyond the strife and pain
Of baffled sense;—no tribute of lament
Above thy futile toil, and grief misspent
Can reach thee now, where from thy high disdain
Thou liest so low. Ah, were not too much given
For thy soul's ransom, would that thou wert free
From thine eternal solace to descend,
Only to tell us what availed to heaven
Thy life of sacrifice and pain, that we
Might know of our self-pleasing years the end.

28

To walk this world with eyes forever cast
On the unsure foundations of its peace,
Will buy of God no favor, nor decrease
The power of evil. From the inviolate past,
The world that is, the shadowed presence vast
Of worlds to come, since nothing can release
The bond of infinite oneness, let us cease
Our ignorant rebellion, nor contrast
Eternity and time, nor life and death,
As though we might escape from death or time
In that "Memento Mori." Though it be
All things are vanity, as the preacher saith,—
Not even mystic faith can make sublime
The impatience of our brief humanity.

29

In life's young consciousness of inborn might
We vow, that in the changes years may bring,
Our hearts shall ever keep their tender spring,
That age shall never steal our young delight.
Let us then know, that of all powers, that wait
An endless warfare with our peace to wage,—
Hastening the current of our youth to age,
No one is stronger, nor more sure than Hate.
Pray that ye hate not, even with zeal of right,
Men who are hateful; lest the power grow,
Until of all the holiest things ye know,
Not one will more be lovely in your sight:
And ye are homeless strangers in your land,
With age and pain and sorrow nigh at hand.

30

WITH this eternal winter in my breast,
Why do these airs of spring-time, and the sound
Of skilful music, wake these hopes profound,
My heart shall have the joy it once possessed!
Such joy can come no more where Fear, before,
In life's clear day his dark device hath spun:
The wrong the cunning of his hand has done,
The hand of Love cannot undo. No more
Need hope disturb my patience, and the powers
That teach me to accept this wise despair,
Must help me not alone the grief to bear,
But all the snares of these Enchanted Bowers,
Where echoes of the past around me pour
Sweet sounds of love, that can return no more.

31

WILL not the omnipotent God bow down the skies
To my importunate prayer? Believe not so;
But set thy soul to learn its task, and know
That all great sorrow, though our nature cries
Aloud for rescue, in its blind surprise,
Is but a part of the eternal flow
Of things that are. No hand, save of the slow
Advancing past, can grant thy prayer. How wise,
He who implores no sign from heaven, how brave,
Who dares not waste his power in vain appeal,
But from the shipwreck of his dearest hope
Whatever may be gathered, seeks to save;
And even from his own heart would fain conceal,
Of that dread loss its wide and desolate scope.

32

WHETHER our virtues be the unconscious fruits
And organism of a balanced mind,
Or whether culture, or the favor blind
Of fair surrounding unto gold transmutes
A native evil, all our grace disputes
Will not determine. And so far declined
The Light that lit the world, how shall we find
Faith to receive the virtue He imputes!
Yet, even though your own birthright be secure
To thrones of heaven, though these laborious days
In your own vineyards, reap immortal gain,
Ah, let the righteousness of Christ endure
For those, on whom inherited failure weighs,
Who have no title of their own to reign.

33

WHAT we must reap, that have we sown. Alas,
That only when our harvest fields are sown,
Do we first know the truth we might have known,
Before the day of reckoning came to pass;
Before the inflexible heavens were as brass
Above our long remorse. Though we atone
To God and man, with tears that do surpass
The measure of our fault, what we have sown,
Remains to be the harvest we must reap;
And though kind Nature still hath peace in store,
And the long solace of the evening years;
Yet even He, who for His wandering sheep,
Laid down His life, can bring lost hope no more,
Nor lift the burden of our midnight tears.

34

CHILD, that awakest from thy mystic's dream,
Whose weary will shall never more aspire
To those far heights, in whom a quenched fire
Of conscience, weary of her star supreme,
Shall light no more,— let not the eternal beam
Of truth, to thee, with that lost hope expire.
Far in the waning heavens of thy desire—
The presence of undying love, the gleam
Of the enduring promise, thy distrust
Could never change. The penance of thy pain,
Thy expedient self-denial, unto Him
Who knows our frame, remembering we are dust,
Are lost indeed;—and thy endurance vain,
And all in vain, but faith, however dim.

35

Ye unto the name of Christ, your Light,
Your King and atoning Savior is so dear,
Who through these mists of time, can see so clear,
The Father's love on Calvary's awful height:—
What offering can be precious in his sight,
What tribute of thanksgiving reach his ear
From you, who judge the souls he loved, nor fear
His secret law of absolute Wrong and Right?
If ye, children of faith, may suffer doubt
And grieve the days wherein his voice is dumb
Within the temple where your offerings wait.—
How know ye not, that ofttimes, far without
The gates of faith, a voice to us may come,
And unbelief's assurance hesitate?

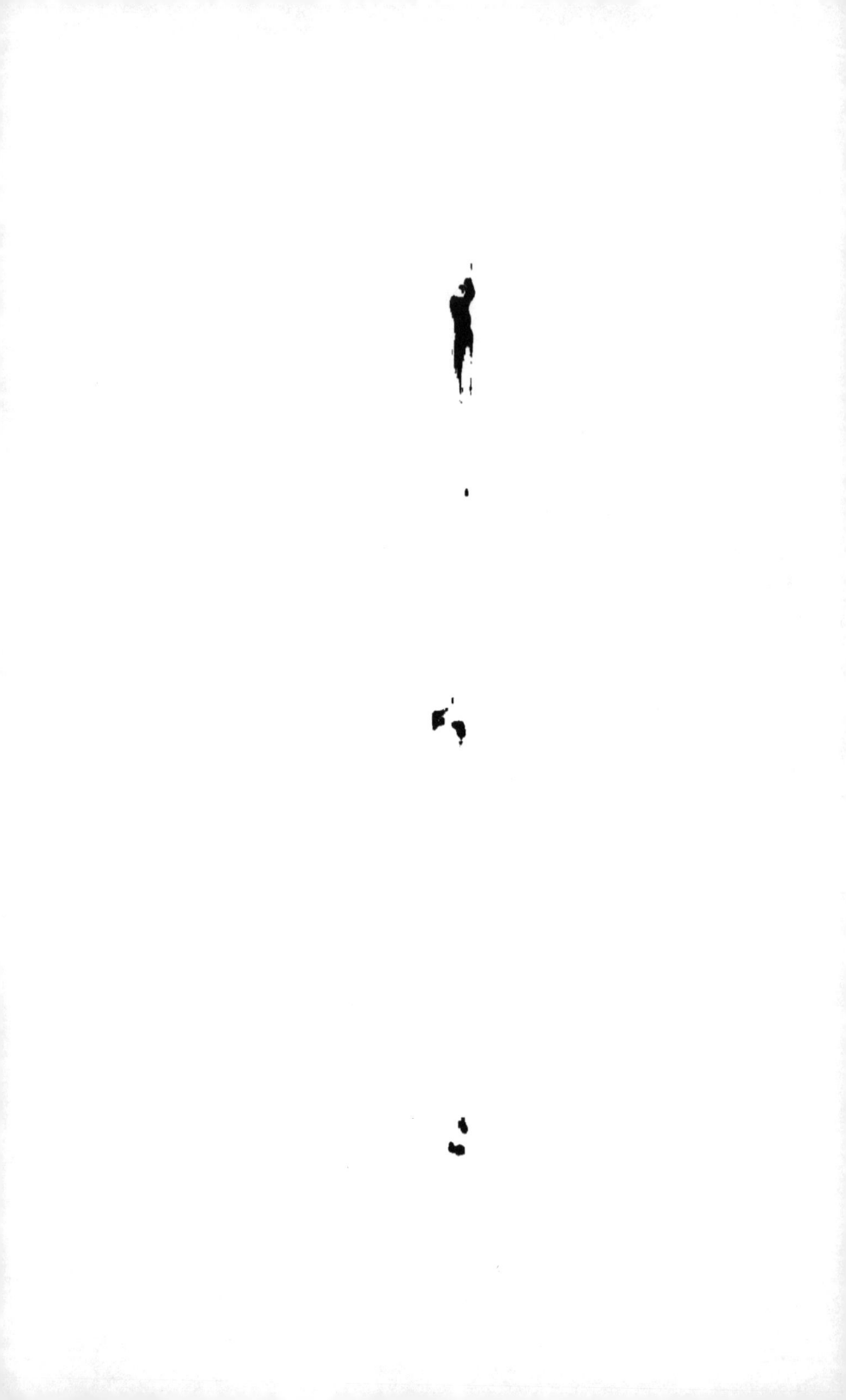

36

AND thou, what dost thou here? my spirit said,
With these disciples of the fold shut in,
Who hast no hope nor fear to theirs akin,
Who art not hungry for their living bread?
If from thy quiet deserts of the dead,
Thou wouldst anew the way of life begin,
What Lamb of God can take away thy sin,
Or give a form to faith whose soul has fled?
Sad spirit,—I know not why thou seest me here,
Only the well-remembered hymn and prayer
I heard again, half reverent, half in scorn;
The unforgotten dream of faith drew near,
And filled these waking moments, with the air
Of some dim Eden, where their light was born.

37

To lie in this dim summer light, with the air
Of ocean in the long sea grass, and flight
Of shining mist above me,— what delight!
I seem a part of Nature's self, and dare,
For these brief moments, to forget my share
In life's great tragedy of Wrong and Right,
Before the listening heavens. On what rare height,
Free from the war of conscience, from despair
Above the irretrievable years, thou reignst,
O Nature,—fair as in the dawn of earth!
Thy storms and whirlwinds never reach thy soul;
While we, forever conquered, fight against
The inevitable limit of our birth,
And learn no lesson from thy self-control.

38

Tomorrow's sun will never shine for thee :
Farewell, O love, for thou must go to-night,
Forever from the darkness and the light!
If this be so, then take away from me
These sounds and sights of earth; and leave me free,
Alone in silence, with the silent night,
That ye may know not when the end may be.
Wilt thou then fear, O soul?— Ye have no right
To watch the anguish of my lingering breath
For answer. Whether seeds of terror, sown
In helpless childhood, spread their shadow drear,
Or the faint light of an immortal death
Prevail above me,— unto me alone
Belongs the hour, whose power is drawing near.

39

THIS night thy soul will be required of thee,
This day thy life shall with the day decline:
If this be so, O, world of love divine!
O, kingdom of my Lord, where I shall see
His face in joy, through love's eternity.
And when your fair tomorrow's sun shall shine,
Although my silent presence make no sign,
Conceive what daylight must have dawned for me,
Where the new glory of God and of the Lamb
Doth make the light. And when at last ye turn
From my cold face, let this assurance burn
Through the dread presence, that the eternal calm
Of truth is mine, and that I hold the key
To your sad problems of humanity.

40

Thy night hast come at last, the starless night
Whose dawn is death. Look forward, soul of mine,
And all possession of thy past resign,—
Thy day of life, whose useless legions fight
In vain. Because thou wilt not yield thy right
To hope and fear that are no longer thine,
Because thou measurest not the strength divine,
Therefore alone the inevitable might
Of death appals thee. Since it is too late
For pleasure, or for deep mistake, or sin,
To barter with thy fears,—let them alone;
And silently advance into the great
Approaching presence, where thou shalt begin
To know thyself as thou wert always known.

41

ALAS for cultured lives, who know so well
The mechanism of souls, who claim to see
So clearly the original decree
That limits Nature's power, they must rebel
In this new paradise where others dwell
Safe in the shadow of the sacred tree
Of infinite life, and are no longer free
To obey the instinct that would faith impel.
Ah, though conviction hath no sovereignty,
Nor man's experience sanction, by the law
Of God's organic world, no lives control
Their springs of faith; and Immortality
Hath power to haunt with superstitious awe
The inward, lonely centre of the soul.

42

When we have given up our young intent
To own the heaven and earth ; when first we know,
That the remorseless years must come and go,
Nor only for ourselves, nor to the bent
Of our desire; that life will not relent
For our mistakes of ignorance, nor bestow
Even a poor martyr name to heal our woe,—
Then first, although our prime of years be spent
Do we begin to live, to know in truth
The hidden depths of mercy; glad of heart
That life and work are left us. Let us pray
For our dear children; that in the strength of youth,
They learn the wisdom we have set apart
Unto the eleventh hour of the day.

43

Oh loving Savior, early I awake,
To call thy name, and in the deep of night,
To thee my soul doth wing her lonely flight,
And live with thee until the morning break.
Each day my soul endureth, for the sake
Of that rare solace, that at times, the sight
Of thine appearance unaware, doth make,—
A sudden dayspring, that resolves in light
All earthly things and heavenly as they are,
And not as men imagine. But how slow
Am I to learn the lesson, than between
Those visions, thou art not withdrawn more far,
Than when thy presence bends the heaven so low,
That earth becomes in turn the world unseen.

44

In guarded pastures have I fed, where weed
Of superstition, nor the cultured flowers
Of sacred dogma grew. The guiding powers
That watched the instincts of my soul to plead
With Heavenly might, kept watch with zealous heed
That I saw not the impregnable walls and towers
Of angered justice, that this world of ours
Has built upon its borders. There did bleed
No Lamb of God for me; and yet, O Christ,
O, pure and lonely martyr undefiled,
Whence is it that now a nameless love is born
Within my soul, before thy sacrificed
And wounded form, thy godlike presence, mild
And silent, in its resurrection morn.

45

THE years were not in vain,—a lifetime, passed
In slow availing prayer to see the alone
Accessible truth, that life could not have known
Through less vicissitude. Revealed at last
The fallacy of that mystic law,—the vast
Unsearchable will of God to make our own,
As though the absolute Glory of his throne
Were at the mercy of his creatures cast;
And fallen the mighty thrones of dogma, wrought
Of human wisdom, superseding law,
By mercy far more legal. Nothing lies
Between the horizon of my earnest thought
And cloudless heavens, where I behold with awe
A sun of inconceivable wisdom rise.

46

My heart is fixed:—henceforth no time, nor place,
Nor power,—no doubt that kills the soul,— no night
Of grievous trial, nor the blinding light
Of the world's day, the moments can efface,
Wherein my soul through mists of time did trace
The Son of Man. Descended from no height
Of cloud built thrones nor crowned in aureole white
Of mystic flame, but with surpassing grace
Of human life,—clear in the Roman past,
His form arose; and I, who saw him, knew
For evermore that this indeed was He,
Whose own received him not,—the First and Last,
The word of God that maketh all things new,
The kingdom and the power and victory.

47

COULDST thou not watch one hour? Alas, he knew
Who kept that loving vigil all alone,
Above a careless world, where even his own,
His dearly loved, slept the long night time through,—
They could not watch. The unwilling sleep that grew
Upon their eyelids, hath more deeply grown
Upon our souls;— no more the sorrowing tone
Of the dear Master can our watch renew.
Choose which of these were life's unhappier fate:—
Back in the current of the world to turn,
With no pretence upon our Lord to wait:
Or to accept the watch, bring oil to burn
Until the morning, but to find at dawn,
That we have slept all night and he has gone.

DEEP virtue hath this cup of healing cold,
Earth's wisdom offers , that however rare
Your life's endurance seem, ye only share
A common fate,—that every heart has told
Your secret of experience, in the old,
And pitiless desert of the heavenly air!
Ah, false and vain! No man can lightlier bear,
That man has borne,—nor earth's arcana hold
A virtue that hath any cure to give
Life's fatal fever. Let us rather face
The outer snow and, ice the Land of Death,
Whereof man knows not, save that God doth live
And rest therein; and from the silent space,
We feel Religion's cold, inspiring breath.

49

OF the stern heaven ye make what hopeless quest!
Freedom to follow your unguided will,
With all the assurance and the power that fill
Those souls alone, that in obedience rest:—
Freedom from loss and sorrow, with that best
And surest knowledge they alone instil:—
The heart of youth, with the unerring skill
To read the whole of life, that is possessed
Through years of insight only. Of mankind
Ye claim as gods, to judge and recompense
The good and evil, while your eyes are blind
To all that lies beyond your narrow sense:
Neither of heaven nor earth ye have the key
Neither in life nor death the victory.

50

IT is no irreverence, friend and priest,
For thine high office, that I cannot choose,
Even in these bonds of friendship, but refuse
Thy gift in ministry, that my need, at least,
Can minister nothing,— though it be a feast
To thousands, that in losing thee, would lose
Their bread of life. Let not thy pride accuse
Just Nature, that some minds she has released
From that lay service, but arraign the blind
Though careful judgment, that through time unknown,
Has failed to sanction that release. O friend,
Thou seest with me two lives divide mankind:
The priest's,— though priest unto himself alone,—
And his who must on priestly help depend.

51

HE is it who hath made us, and not we
Ourselves; and in one human mould is cast,—
Though with discerning justice we contrast
Our lives with others,— all humanity
He is not from the bonds of Nature free,
Who wills to be in lonely priesthood classed;
The slowest years will manifest at last
The tether of his vaunted liberty.
For pierced by secret sin, and weak with pain,
Or worn with long vicissitude of fate,
The organism of his weary brain,
Will fear or superstition penetrate:
And he the nearest guide will fain receive,
And by a stranger's hope and faith believe.

52

THE inmost veil of heaven is rent in twain,—
Thy Lord is dead, and death has claimed his own;
The seal shall not be broken on the stone,
Nor the stone lifted where thou hast him lain.
Hadst thou had faith but as this living grain,
He would have lived:—but lost in death, unknown,
He sleepeth; and unto the Father's throne
The son of man will never rise again.
Now art thou strong: and thou hast need of strength,
Lest in thy plastic conscience, clear and still,
The impress of his beauty should remain,
To haunt the friendless years, and light at length
The spark of dread conviction in thy will:—
"This was the Son of God that I have slain."

53

THAT thou hast reached the height of mortal joy,
Boast not of life, as though thy joy were all
Of human fate, or griefs that elsewhere fall,
Like arrows in the soul, could life destroy.
Earth will outlast our pleasure and our pain;
And only after many peaceful years,
And many days and nights of anxious tears,
Can we look back, and count our loss and gain.
Then may we claim indeed a favored lot,
If of our keenest grief we knew the worst;
If in our hearts no lingering doubt is nursed,
No unexplained misgivings, unforgot,
Can mar the peace experience brings to life,
With distant murmur of perpetual strife.

54

WHAT serves the illusion of thy restless mind
That life can be uncertain of its fate?
Although thy weak self-mercy vacillate
From wise despair, to longings undefined
That have the form of hope, thou hast divined
The secret truth. Uncertainty can wait
Not long upon our pleasure, nor create
Such hope as may the inward vision blind.
Thou knowest the worst: the best is still to learn:—
The boundless power of life to adjust her course
To final truth, without the heart's consent.
All things that earth has given, to earth return,
And youth will die, but life's undying force
Upon her fair amenities be spent.

55

MAN is a race of kings. Who that is born,
Feels not that he should have been born to rule!
Nor was designed to be the pliant tool
Of inclination, in allegiance sworn
To Nature—cruel master! Ah so shorn
Of that fair grace of kingship, in what school
Shall he attain the knowledge how to rule,
And live no longer prey of his self scorn?
There is indeed a talismanic word,
That holds the gate of power and liberty,—
The word Obedience, but its magic sound,
Lost in familiar language, is unheard,
Its power unknown, to us who seek the key
Whereby dominion of the earth is found.

56

For that fair morn of youth,—the discipline
Of happy years, that hath its uses stern,
No less than sorrow's self, our hearts return
A twofold gratitude. Had life not been
The sum of all possession earth could win,
Her highest lesson had remained to learn.
With God's elect, the passionate fires that burn
Their youth to dust, are but that fire within,
Where the Refiner sits; and as from dross
Glimmers the gold, so faith in Jesus Christ
From the dark alchemy of Nature springs;
And they are born again. The ordeal of loss
To acheive the perfect work had not sufficed
Without the wisdom earth's fruition brings.

57

Is it not written :— he that will do His will
Shall know his doctrine? Do not words like these
Pour light above thy conscience, that it sees
The narrow highway, winding clear and still?
"Ah no;—before all things availeth skill
Of teaching, for obedience cannot please
A conscience doubtful of its own decrees
And swayed by Nature:—and no man, until
Conviction of the perfect truth, can know
The perfect will." Not so darest thou reply
Before the courts of heaven; for deep below
The currents of our faltering judgments,lie
The pure decisions of Eternal right,
The will of God, clear in the inward light.

58

WHY should the sunlight and the moonlight shine
And idle mirth and music have their way,
And youth and maiden boast their holiday
With song and laughter, while such grief as mine
Is in the world,—pain that no help, divine
Or human, hath the science to allay!
Ah, be thy source of sorrow what it may,
The world has seen a deeper grief than thine;
For there are souls whose anguish doth so weigh
Her weight upon them, that the careless play
Of life they see not, nor their ears incline
To happy voices ;—or they sadly say:—
Let music and rejoicing have their way
Because the world contains such grief as mine.

59

Our Duty hath no treasure held in store:
The happiness of every hour depends
Upon the hope and confidence she sends,
The wages of an hour gone before.
This life's continual toil can earn no more
Than to buy oil, the lamp of Duty spends;
Her yesterday a guiding ray extends,
But can the strength to follow not restore.
They who accept her service to beguile
An aching heart, will find a sure reward
In serving, but if for a little while
Their tired wills should rest, the cold regard
Of Duty will disown them, and the old pain
Unchecked of passive conscience, must remain.

60

THE rigorous law that measures punishment
To our unconscious sins, without regard
To helpless inexperience, or the hard
Conditions of perfection, was not sent
With the unequal justice of intent,
To punish only, but to assure and guard
For our unwilling virtues, more reward
Than waits their true deserving. One who hath
His years in toils of stern necessity,   [spent
Or selfish virtue, sees the unloved restraint
Compel a gradual patience in his soul;
And finds the triumph born of Self-control,
Silence the ignoble wailing of complaint,—
And that in true subjection, he is free.

61

O RESTLESS Shepherd's dog, that up and down
Pursuest thy Master's sheep, art thou so sure
Thou knowest the greenest fold, the spring most pure
For every lamb? What floods so ever drown,
What beasts devour, what pastures dry and brown
May starve the flock, or hidden snare allure
In many a tempting shelter insecure,—
Thou hast no heed save of thine own renown
For zealous service. Will, not at thy hands,
The Shepherd of his flock demand the sheep
That thou hast led from many a sheltered fold
Of early faith, at last to treacherous sands
Of dogma, whereon pours the unsounded deep
Of faithless human reason, dark and cold.

62

Ruskin,— the fruitless logic of thy course
To that rare sympathy doth make appeal
Of those elect children of men, who feel
The grave relations of the eternal force
Of art to life. Thou, who the hidden source
Of perfect beauty wouldst to men unseal,
The imperfection that no art can heal,
Didst slowly learn, with how sublime remorse.
Others have seen creation's curse with thee,
And felt the burden of the earth no less;
But from their cultured ease, few lives would dare
With thine, embark upon the hopeless sea
Of human ills, or even at heart confess
How nobler far thy hope, than their despair.

63

SHALL I be startled at the cry: "Prepare
To meet thy God?" To me the thought doth bring
Enduring consolation;—not the sting
Of terror in the conscious heart, laid bare
Before the world that cannot weigh nor spare.
O infinite Father of my life, O King
And Judge,— be thine in everything
The judgment and the sentence. Every prayer
Of the wakeful night goes up before thee, all
The elements that wrought our being's laws
Were woven in thy presence, and no chain
Of motives, but thy mercy shall recall,
Thy justice weigh, when thou shalt plead our cause,
Nor tax our ignorant conscience to explain.

64

THE long disquiet of thy soul's estate,—
The fretful passion, and the nameless pain
That haunts the triumph of our fairest gain
Comes from no malice of celestial fate,
But that the eternal truth has dawned too late,—
Ye cannot serve two Masters. Ye remain
In half allegiance to the exacting reign
Of truth, the loving master, stern and great,
While every moment brings its petty weight
Of social bondage, falsehoods that restrain
From loyal action, courteous words that feign
A willing service to the world ye hate.
Renounce that world,—or from high truth refrain;
And neither master shall ye serve in vain

65

THOU art avenged, dear child, for any wrong,
I, knowing or unknowing, might have done;
No penance were more deep, than thus to long
To see thy face once more beneath the sun.
Yet not to him whose childish years belong
To me, who saw their happy moments run,
Dare we look more;— but unto thee, thou strong
And silent Angel! who hast now begun
The eternal years of God. Oh, child and saint
Remember us, we pray thee, who remain
Here, where no light of knowledge comes, who faint
Beneath the hope and faith that are so vain.
Thy little grave lies dark in the outer night;
Thine angel lost on some cold shining height.

www.ingramcontent.com/pod-product-compliance
Lightning Source LLC
Chambersburg PA
CBHW022336020726
47500CB00004B/1146